Crossing Brooklyn Ferry

*Time, Connection & Urban Beauty in
a Lyrical Journey Across the Water*

A Modern Translation
Adapted for the Contemporary Reader

Walt Whitman

Translated by Tim Zengerink

Table of Contents

Preface
Message to the Reader

Rebuilding the Greatest Library in Human History

Thousands of years ago, the Library of Alexandria was the heart of global knowledge — a sanctuary where the wisdom of every known civilization was gathered and shared freely.

And then, it was lost.

Now, we're rebuilding it — and you are invited to join us.

At the Library of Alexandria, we've set out to make every book available to every person on Earth — not just in print, but in every language, every format, and for every reader.

Here's how we do it:

- **Deluxe Print Editions at True Printing Cost** - Order any book as a high-quality paperback, elegant hardcover, or stunning boxset — and only pay what it costs to print. No markups. No middlemen.
- **Unlimited Access to the Greatest Works** - Enjoy thousands of timeless classics — from Plato to Shakespeare to Tolstoy — in beautiful, modern eBook and audiobook editions. Read and listen without limits — for every reader, everywhere.
- **Modern Translations for Every Language & Dialect** - We're reimagining the classics in clear, accessible language — and translating them into every dialect imaginable. Everyone deserves to understand humanity's greatest ideas.

When you visit **LibraryofAlexandria.com**, you're not just accessing books — you're joining a global movement to restore, preserve, and share the wisdom of civilization.

Join us today at LibraryofAlexandria.com

Together, we'll ensure the light of human wisdom never fades again.

With gratitude,

The Modern Library of Alexandria Team

Visit:
www.libraryofalexandria.com
Or scan the code below:

Introduction

Walt Whitman's Vision
of Eternal Human Kinship

Walt Whitman's *Crossing Brooklyn Ferry* stands as one of the most profound meditations on time, identity, and the interconnectedness of human beings ever penned in the English language. First appearing in the 1856 edition of *Leaves of Grass* under the title *Sun-Down Poem* before assuming its more iconic name, this work is both lyrical and philosophical, intimate and panoramic. Set on a ferry ride between Brooklyn and Manhattan—then a daily ritual for thousands and now a metaphor for human continuity—the poem becomes an expansive reflection on shared experience, universal emotions, and the poetic power of place.

Whitman transforms the simple act of crossing a body of water into a grand metaphysical passage, a metaphorical traversal of eras and psyches. With every lapping wave and swirl of the tide, he touches upon the eternal human condition—our loneliness, our longing, our joy, our fears, and the deep thread of unity that binds us despite time's passage. The ferry becomes a floating stage upon which past, present, and future riders converge. For Whitman, those who come after him are not strangers or abstractions—they are his siblings, his companions, his very self extended forward in time.

Few poets before or since have attempted with such vigor to collapse the distance between speaker and reader, present and future, flesh and soul. In *Crossing Brooklyn Ferry*, Whitman does not simply describe a moment; he inhabits it in such a way that it expands beyond its own temporal borders. He anticipates our reading. He gazes across generations. He refuses to be locked into the past or buried under the weight of history. Instead, he steps forward, hand extended, calling us to recognize our shared humanity, our common urban rhythms, our mutual fears and delights.

The poem is both deeply rooted in place and astonishingly universal. New York City—its people, light, water, and chaos—shapes the texture of the work. But the ideas it contains transcend geography. Whether one has crossed the East River or not, whether one has seen the sun set behind tall buildings or has never touched the steel of a ferry rail, Whitman's vision embraces all who have stood at the threshold between solitude and connection. His poem pulses with life and humanity in every line.

This introduction will guide readers through the historical context, structural innovations, and spiritual depths of *Crossing Brooklyn Ferry*, offering an enriched lens for experiencing the poem as a living conversation across time. It is not a relic but a companion. A reader who enters into Whitman's waters does not simply observe; they participate, becoming one of the "many thousands" the poet lovingly addresses. This is not poetry for passive consumption—it is an invocation, an embrace, an initiation into a greater human family.

Merging Past, Present, and Future

One of the most remarkable features of *Crossing Brooklyn Ferry* is its fluidity in time. The poem begins with a precise, almost photographic scene: the poet aboard a ferry, watching the sun descend as the vessel makes its slow journey across the East River. Yet within moments, this particular sunset becomes every sunset. The passengers on board become every person who has ever made the crossing—and every reader who will encounter the poem. The ferry ride becomes a ritual of communion not only with the physical world, but with the entire human lineage that has ever felt, seen, or dreamed.

Whitman's speaker does not merely witness; he transcends. He writes:

"It avails not, time nor place—distance avails not,

I am with you, you men and women of a generation, or ever so many generations hence…"

With these lines, he obliterates linear temporality. The speaker becomes both historical and eternal. He affirms that the same emotions—the same glances, worries, passions, and hungers—animate all people, regardless of their century or station. This is not an abstract hope; it is a radical claim. For Whitman, poetry is the vehicle by which souls can meet across time, unhindered by the body's limitations or the world's boundaries.

This idea is not only innovative but revolutionary. In a culture often obsessed with progress and the new, Whitman insists on the recurrence of emotion and experience. He finds holiness in repetition, divinity in the mundane. Each ferry ride is different, yet also the same. Each generation carries its own burdens, yet also echoes the struggles and triumphs of those who came before. He invites the reader to see themselves as part of a larger human organism, linked not just by blood or geography but by shared inner life.

The poet's transcendence of time is mirrored in the structure of the poem itself. It lacks a conventional narrative arc. Instead, it flows like the river it describes—moving steadily, sometimes swelling with intensity, sometimes drifting into meditative stillness. The repetition of key phrases—such as "just as you feel when you look on the river and sky, so I felt"—acts as a rhythmic pulse, reinforcing the idea that emotional truth is a constant, echoing across eras like ripples on water.

This temporal flattening serves a spiritual purpose. Whitman constructs a form of immortality not based on fame or divine judgment, but on presence. He assures us that we are not alone—that even if the faces around us change, even if our cities evolve and our technologies replace the ferry with bridges and subways, the soul beneath remains familiar. In this way, the poem becomes a kind of scripture for modern humanity: a text that declares not separation, but oneness. Not decay, but continuity.

The Sacred in the Cityscape

If Whitman's temporal vision is expansive, his geographic one is equally revolutionary. At a time when romantic poetry often looked to nature—mountains, lakes, forests—for spiritual inspiration, Whitman found the divine in the very heart of the city. *Crossing Brooklyn Ferry* is a love letter to urban life, a sacred chant woven from the smoke, noise, motion, and humanity of nineteenth-century New York.

Far from being alienated by the crush of the city, Whitman finds solace and beauty in its rhythms. He observes the crowds with joy, not suspicion. He watches the buildings with awe, not dread. The ferry itself is a vessel of democracy—its deck filled with people of all kinds, united in motion and moment. In this floating liminal space, he sees the potential for spiritual awakening. The river becomes not merely a body of water, but a threshold to understanding.

He writes:

"Closer yet I approach you,

What thought you have of me now, I had as much of you—I laid in my stores in advance…"

Here, Whitman not only addresses the future reader but enacts a kind of intimacy rarely found in poetry. He suggests that the separation between self and other, between city dwellers and country walkers, between past and future, is illusory. The poem becomes a dialogue—not with God, not with history, but with us.

This approach to urban spirituality is not naïve or escapist. Whitman acknowledges the darkness of city life— its struggles, its anonymity, its mechanical indifference. He speaks of "the curious abrupt questionings," "the doubts of day-time and the doubts of night-time," and "the dark patches." Yet even in this acknowledgment, there is no despair. The darkness is not a void, but a veil. Through it, the shared humanity of the city's dwellers becomes more visible, not less.

In this way, *Crossing Brooklyn Ferry* functions as a deeply mystical text. It insists that every aspect of human experience—light and dark, pleasure and pain, solitude and community—is worthy of reverence. The ferry ride becomes a ritual passage, the city a sacred landscape, the crowd a congregation. The spiritual is not above or beyond the urban—it is inside it, pulsing with life, carried in the breath of every commuter, etched into the steel of the ferry's hull.

Whitman's genius lies in his ability to transform the ordinary into the transcendent. He invites us to see our commutes, our neighborhoods, our casual glances and private doubts as part of a vast, ongoing hymn. He teaches us that beauty is not a fixed aesthetic, but a way of seeing. To cross the Brooklyn Ferry with Whitman is to be inducted into a new kind of seeing—a vision that turns bridges into altars and fellow passengers into saints.

As you prepare to immerse yourself in *Crossing Brooklyn Ferry*, take a moment to pause and reflect. The poem you are about to read is not just about a place or a moment; it is about you. Whitman wrote it for you, anticipated your reading, and believed in your kinship with him across the divide of time. Let yourself be moved by the current of his words, let yourself be seen in his lines, and let yourself be transformed—not by grand revelations, but by the slow unfolding of shared feeling.

Whitman's ferry continues to cross, not just between Brooklyn and Manhattan, but between souls, between centuries, between solitude and communion. Step aboard. The journey is yours now.

Crossing Brooklyn Ferry

1

Flood-tide below me! I see you face to face!
Clouds of the west—sun there half an hour high—I see you also face
to face.

Crowds of men and women attired in the usual costumes, how curious
you are to me!
On the ferry-boats the hundreds and hundreds that cross, returning
home, are more curious to me than you suppose,
And you that shall cross from shore to shore years hence are more
to me, and more in my meditations, than you might suppose.

2

The impalpable sustenance of me from all things at all hours of the day,
The simple, compact, well-join'd scheme, myself disintegrated, every
one disintegrated yet part of the scheme,
The similitudes of the past and those of the future,
The glories strung like beads on my smallest sights and hearings, on
the walk in the street and the passage over the river,
The current rushing so swiftly and swimming with me far away,
The others that are to follow me, the ties between me and them,
The certainty of others, the life, love, sight, hearing of others.

Others will enter the gates of the ferry and cross from shore to shore,
Others will watch the run of the flood-tide,
Others will see the shipping of Manhattan north and west, and the
heights of Brooklyn to the south and east,

Others will see the islands large and small;
Fifty years hence, others will see them as they cross, the sun half
an hour high,
A hundred years hence, or ever so many hundred years hence, others
will see them,
Will enjoy the sunset, the pouring-in of the flood-tide, the
falling-back to the sea of the ebb-tide.

3

It avails not, time nor place—distance avails not,
I am with you, you men and women of a generation, or ever so many
generations hence,
Just as you feel when you look on the river and sky, so I felt,
Just as any of you is one of a living crowd, I was one of a crowd,
Just as you are refresh'd by the gladness of the river and the
bright flow, I was refresh'd,
Just as you stand and lean on the rail, yet hurry with the swift
current, I stood yet was hurried,
Just as you look on the numberless masts of ships and the
thick-stemm'd pipes of steamboats, I look'd.

I too many and many a time cross'd the river of old,
Watched the Twelfth-month sea-gulls, saw them high in the air
floating with motionless wings, oscillating their bodies,
Saw how the glistening yellow lit up parts of their bodies and left
the rest in strong shadow,
Saw the slow-wheeling circles and the gradual edging toward the south,
Saw the reflection of the summer sky in the water,
Had my eyes dazzled by the shimmering track of beams,
Look'd at the fine centrifugal spokes of light round the shape of my
head in the sunlit water,
Look'd on the haze on the hills southward and south-westward,

Look'd on the vapor as it flew in fleeces tinged with violet,
Look'd toward the lower bay to notice the vessels arriving,
Saw their approach, saw aboard those that were near me,
Saw the white sails of schooners and sloops, saw the ships at anchor,
The sailors at work in the rigging or out astride the spars,
The round masts, the swinging motion of the hulls, the slender serpentine pennants,
The large and small steamers in motion, the pilots in their pilothouses,
The white wake left by the passage, the quick tremulous whirl of the wheels,
The flags of all nations, the falling of them at sunset,
The scallop-edged waves in the twilight, the ladled cups, the frolic-some crests and glistening,
The stretch afar growing dimmer and dimmer, the gray walls of the granite storehouses by the docks,
On the river the shadowy group, the big steam-tug closely flank'd on each side by the barges, the hay-boat, the belated lighter,
On the neighboring shore the fires from the foundry chimneys burning high and glaringly into the night,
Casting their flicker of black contrasted with wild red and yellow light over the tops of houses, and down into the clefts of streets.

4

These and all else were to me the same as they are to you,
I loved well those cities, loved well the stately and rapid river,
The men and women I saw were all near to me,
Others the same—others who look back on me because I look'd forward
to them,
  (The time will come, though I stop here to-day and to-night.)

5

What is it then between us?
What is the count of the scores or hundreds of years between us?

Whatever it is, it avails not—distance avails not, and place avails not,
I too lived, Brooklyn of ample hills was mine,
I too walk'd the streets of Manhattan island, and bathed in the waters around it,
I too felt the curious abrupt questionings stir within me,
In the day among crowds of people sometimes they came upon me,
In my walks home late at night or as I lay in my bed they came upon me,
I too had been struck from the float forever held in solution,
I too had receiv'd identity by my body,
That I was I knew was of my body, and what I should be I knew I should be of my body.

6

It is not upon you alone the dark patches fall,
The dark threw its patches down upon me also,
The best I had done seem'd to me blank and suspicious,
My great thoughts as I supposed them, were they not in reality meagre?
Nor is it you alone who know what it is to be evil,
I am he who knew what it was to be evil,
I too knitted the old knot of contrariety,
Blabb'd, blush'd, resented, lied, stole, grudg'd,
Had guile, anger, lust, hot wishes I dared not speak,
Was wayward, vain, greedy, shallow, sly, cowardly, malignant,
The wolf, the snake, the hog, not wanting in me.
The cheating look, the frivolous word, the adulterous wish, not wanting,
Refusals, hates, postponements, meanness, laziness, none of these

wanting,
Was one with the rest, the days and haps of the rest,
Was call'd by my nighest name by clear loud voices of young men as
they saw me approaching or passing,
Felt their arms on my neck as I stood, or the negligent leaning of
their flesh against me as I sat,
Saw many I loved in the street or ferry-boat or public assembly, yet
never told them a word,
Lived the same life with the rest, the same old laughing, gnawing,
sleeping,
Play'd the part that still looks back on the actor or actress,
The same old role, the role that is what we make it, as great as we like,
Or as small as we like, or both great and small.

7

Closer yet I approach you,
What thought you have of me now, I had as much of you—I laid in
my
stores in advance,
I consider'd long and seriously of you before you were born.

Who was to know what should come home to me?
Who knows but I am enjoying this?
Who knows, for all the distance, but I am as good as looking at you
now, for all you cannot see me?

8

Ah, what can ever be more stately and admirable to me than
mast-hemm'd Manhattan?
River and sunset and scallop-edg'd waves of flood-tide?
The sea-gulls oscillating their bodies, the hay-boat in the

twilight, and the belated lighter?
What gods can exceed these that clasp me by the hand,
and with voices I
love call me promptly and loudly by my nighest name as approach?
What is more subtle than this which ties me to the woman or man that
looks in my face?
Which fuses me into you now, and pours my meaning into you?

We understand then do we not?
What I promis'd without mentioning it, have you not accepted?
What the study could not teach—what the preaching could not
accomplish is accomplish'd, is it not?

9

Flow on, river! flow with the flood-tide, and ebb with the ebb-tide!
Frolic on, crested and scallop-edg'd waves!
Gorgeous clouds of the sunset! drench with your splendor me, or the
men and women generations after me!
Cross from shore to shore, countless crowds of passengers!
Stand up, tall masts of Mannahatta! stand up, beautiful hills of
Brooklyn!
Throb, baffled and curious brain! throw out questions and answers!
Suspend here and everywhere, eternal float of solution!
Gaze, loving and thirsting eyes, in the house or street or public assembly!
Sound out, voices of young men! loudly and musically call me by my
nighest name!
Live, old life! play the part that looks back on the actor or actress!
Play the old role, the role that is great or small according as one
makes it!
Consider, you who peruse me, whether I may not in unknown ways be
looking upon you;
Be firm, rail over the river, to support those who lean idly, yet

haste with the hasting current;

Fly on, sea-birds! fly sideways, or wheel in large circles high in the air;

Receive the summer sky, you water, and faithfully hold it till all downcast eyes have time to take it from you!

Diverge, fine spokes of light, from the shape of my head, or any one's head, in the sunlit water!

Come on, ships from the lower bay! pass up or down, white-sail'd schooners, sloops, lighters!

Flaunt away, flags of all nations! be duly lower'd at sunset!

Burn high your fires, foundry chimneys! cast black shadows at nightfall! cast red and yellow light over the tops of the houses!

Appearances, now or henceforth, indicate what you are,

You necessary film, continue to envelop the soul,

About my body for me, and your body for you, be hung our divinest aromas,

Thrive, cities—bring your freight, bring your shows, ample and sufficient rivers,

Expand, being than which none else is perhaps more spiritual,

Keep your places, objects than which none else is more lasting.

You have waited, you always wait, you dumb, beautiful ministers,

We receive you with free sense at last, and are insatiate henceforward,

Not you any more shall be able to foil us, or withhold yourselves from us,

We use you, and do not cast you aside—we plant you permanently within us,

We fathom you not—we love you—there is perfection in you also,

You furnish your parts toward eternity,

Great or small, you furnish your parts toward the soul.

Song of the Answerer

1

Now list to my morning's romanza, I tell the signs of the Answerer,
To the cities and farms I sing as they spread in the sunshine before me.

A young man comes to me bearing a message from his brother,
How shall the young man know the whether and when of his brother?
Tell him to send me the signs. And I stand before the young man
face to face, and take his right hand in my left hand and his
left hand in my right hand,
And I answer for his brother and for men, and I answer for him that
answers for all, and send these signs.

Him all wait for, him all yield up to, his word is decisive and final,
Him they accept, in him lave, in him perceive themselves as amid light,
Him they immerse and he immerses them.

Beautiful women, the haughtiest nations, laws, the landscape,
people, animals,
The profound earth and its attributes and the unquiet ocean, (so
tell I my morning's romanza,)
All enjoyments and properties and money, and whatever money will
buy,
The best farms, others toiling and planting and he unavoidably reaps,
The noblest and costliest cities, others grading and building and he
domiciles there,
Nothing for any one but what is for him, near and far are for him,
the ships in the offing,

The perpetual shows and marches on land are for him
if they are for anybody.

He puts things in their attitudes,
He puts to-day out of himself with plasticity and love,
He places his own times, reminiscences, parents, brothers and
sisters, associations, employment, politics, so that the rest
never shame them afterward, nor assume to command them.

He is the Answerer,
What can be answer'd he answers, and what cannot be answer'd he
shows how it cannot be answer'd.

A man is a summons and challenge,
 (It is vain to skulk—do you hear that mocking and laughter? do you
hear the ironical echoes?)

Books, friendships, philosophers, priests, action, pleasure, pride,
beat up and down seeking to give satisfaction,
He indicates the satisfaction, and indicates them that beat up and
down also.

Whichever the sex, whatever the season or place, he may go freshly
and gently and safely by day or by night,
He has the pass-key of hearts, to him the response of the prying of
hands on the knobs.

His welcome is universal, the flow of beauty is not more welcome or
universal than he is,
The person he favors by day or sleeps with at night is blessed.

Every existence has its idiom, every thing has an idiom and tongue,
He resolves all tongues into his own and bestows it upon men, and
any man translates, and any man translates himself also,
One part does not counteract another part, he is the joiner, he sees
how they join.

He says indifferently and alike How are you friend? to the President
at his levee,
And he says Good-day my brother, to Cudge that hoes in the sugar-
field,
And both understand him and know that his speech is right.

He walks with perfect ease in the capitol,
He walks among the Congress, and one Representative says to another,
Here is our equal appearing and new.

Then the mechanics take him for a mechanic,
And the soldiers suppose him to be a soldier, and the sailors that
he has follow'd the sea,
And the authors take him for an author, and the artists for an artist,
And the laborers perceive he could labor with them and love them,
No matter what the work is, that he is the one to follow it or has
follow'd it,
No matter what the nation, that he might find his brothers and
sisters there.

The English believe he comes of their English stock,
A Jew to the Jew he seems, a Russ to the Russ, usual and near,
removed from none.

Whoever he looks at in the traveler's coffee-house claims him,
The Italian or Frenchman is sure, the German is sure, the Spaniard
is sure, and the island Cuban is sure,

The engineer, the deck-hand on the great lakes, or on the Mississippi
or St. Lawrence or Sacramento, or Hudson or Paumanok sound,
claims him.

The gentleman of perfect blood acknowledges his perfect blood,
The insulter, the prostitute, the angry person, the beggar, see
themselves in the ways of him, he strangely transmutes them,
They are not vile any more, they hardly know themselves they are so
grown.

2

The indications and tally of time,
Perfect sanity shows the master among philosophs,
Time, always without break, indicates itself in parts,
What always indicates the poet is the crowd of the pleasant company
of singers, and their words,
The words of the singers are the hours or minutes of the light or dark,
but the words of the maker of poems are the general light and dark,
The maker of poems settles justice, reality, immortality,
His insight and power encircle things and the human race,
He is the glory and extract thus far of things and of the human race.

The singers do not beget, only the Poet begets,
The singers are welcom'd, understood, appear often enough, but rare
has the day been, likewise the spot, of the birth of the maker
of poems, the Answerer,
 (Not every century nor every five centuries has contain'd such a
day, for all its names.)

The singers of successive hours of centuries may have ostensible
names, but the name of each of them is one of the singers,
The name of each is, eye-singer, ear-singer, head-singer,

sweet-singer, night-singer, parlor-singer, love-singer,
weird-singer, or something else.

All this time and at all times wait the words of true poems,
The words of true poems do not merely please,
The true poets are not followers of beauty but the august masters of beauty;
The greatness of sons is the exuding of the greatness of mothers and fathers,
The words of true poems are the tuft and final applause of science.

Divine instinct, breadth of vision, the law of reason, health, rudeness of body, withdrawnness,
Gayety, sun-tan, air-sweetness, such are some of the words of poems.

The sailor and traveler underlie the maker of poems, the Answerer,
The builder, geometer, chemist, anatomist, phrenologist, artist, all these underlie the maker of poems, the Answerer.

The words of the true poems give you more than poems,
They give you to form for yourself poems, religions, politics, war, peace, behavior, histories, essays, daily life, and every thing else,
They balance ranks, colors, races, creeds, and the sexes,
They do not seek beauty, they are sought,
Forever touching them or close upon them follows beauty, longing, fain, love-sick.

They prepare for death, yet are they not the finish, but rather the outset,
They bring none to his or her terminus or to be content and full,
Whom they take they take into space to behold the birth of stars, to learn one of the meanings,
To launch off with absolute faith, to sweep through the ceaseless rings and never be quiet again.

Thank You For Reading

You've Just Read a Piece of the Greatest Library Ever Rebuilt

Thank you for reading.

This book is one of thousands we're restoring, reimagining, and translating as part of the **Modern Library of Alexandria** — a global movement to preserve and share humanity's most important ideas.

What was once lost to fire and time is now rising again — not just as memory, but as living, breathing knowledge, freely accessible to all.

What You Can Do Next:

- **Keep Reading.**

   Discover more legendary works — in beautiful print, audiobook, or digital form — at LibraryofAlexandria.com.

- **Build Your Own Library.**

   Every title is available as a paperback, hardcover, or collectible boxset — at true printing cost. Craft a personal library worthy of display.

- **Spread the Light.**

   Share this book. Tell others about the movement. Help us translate every timeless work into every language, so no reader is ever left behind.

By finishing this book, you've already taken part in something extraordinary.

Join us at LibraryofAlexandria.com

Together, we're rebuilding the greatest library the world has ever known.

With appreciation,

The Modern Library of Alexandria Team

Visit:
www.libraryofalexandria.com
Or scan the code below: